Zadie
the Sewing
Fairy

by Daisy Meadows

ORCHARD

www.rainbowmagic.co.uk

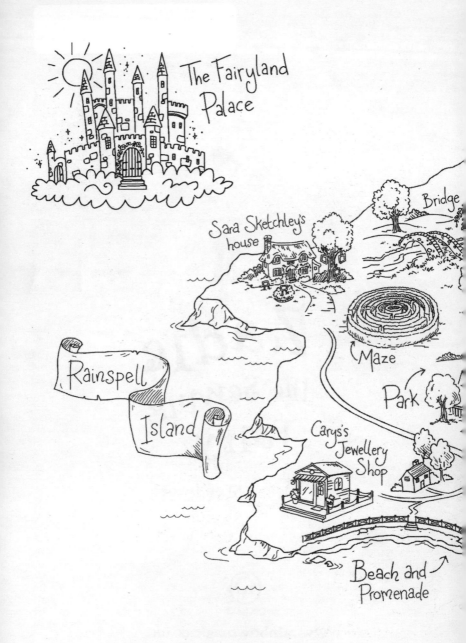

The Fairyland Palace

Sara Sketchley's house

Bridge

Rainspell

Island

Maze

Park

Carys's Jewellery Shop

Beach and Promenade

Jack Frost's
Ice Castle

Campsite

Girls'
tent

Market Square

Mimosa
Cottage

Pottery Hall

Sunshine
Cake Shoppe

Polly Painterly's Workshop

Jack Frost's Spell

I'm a wonderful painter, you must have heard of me,
Marvel at my amazing artistic ability!
With palette, brush and paints in hand,
I'll be the most famous artist in the land!

The Magical Crafts Fairies can't stop me,
I'll steal their magic and then you'll see
That everyone, whatever the cost,
Will want a painting by Jack Frost!

Contents

All Fingers and Thumbs

"It's another magical morning, Kirsty," Rachel said, gazing out of the window of Mimosa Cottage. Although it was still quite early, the sun was already shining, and Rainspell Island looked green and beautiful with the morning light glinting on the sea.

"Do you mean the weather, or our adventures with the Magical Crafts Fairies?" Kirsty asked, her eyes twinkling. They'd arrived on Rainspell two days ago and the girls were taking it in turns to spend one night in Kirsty's quaint little attic bedroom at the B&B with the Tates, and then one night with Rachel's parents at a nearby campsite. The girls loved holidaying on Rainspell Island because it was where they'd first become friends with the fairies.

"A little bit of both!" Rachel replied. "Wasn't it *mean* of Jack Frost to steal all the fairies' magical objects?"

Kirsty nodded. "It was terrible," she agreed, "Especially with Crafts Week here on Rainspell *and* Magical Crafts Week happening at the same time in

Fairyland. No one will have fun doing arts and crafts if Jack Frost has his way!"

While eagerly checking out the Crafts Week activities, Rachel and Kirsty had been thrilled to meet Kayla the Pottery Fairy, one of the seven Magical Crafts Fairies. Kayla had invited them to Fairyland to see King Oberon and Queen Titania announce the opening of Magical Crafts Week. The best and most beautiful crafts produced by the fairies would decorate the Fairyland Palace, so everyone, including the girls, had been very excited.

But the opening ceremony had turned to chaos when Jack Frost and his naughty goblins turned up and threw balloons filled with bright green paint at the crowd. Queen Titania, Kayla and

the other Magical Crafts Fairies had
been splattered with paint and, in the
confusion, Jack Frost and the goblins
had snatched all of the Magical Crafts
Fairies' special objects.

Jack Frost had arrogantly declared
that he was the best at every kind of
craft, and no one else was allowed to
be better than him. Then, with a wave
of his ice wand, he and his goblins had
disappeared to hide in the human world,
taking the magical crafts objects with
them. Rachel and Kirsty knew that
without these special objects the Crafts
Weeks on Rainspell and in Fairyland
would be a complete disaster, so they'd
immediately offered to help the Magical
Crafts Fairies find the goblins and
retrieve the stolen items.

"Doing the pottery and drawing classes was fun, wasn't it?" Kirsty remarked as she buttoned her favourite pink shirt. "But only because we found Kayla's magical vase and Annabelle's magical pencil sharpener just in time."

"And we'll do our best to find the other magical objects, too," Rachel said in a determined voice. "We *can't* let Jack Frost spoil everything!"

13

At that moment Mrs Tate opened the door. "Girls, are you ready for breakfast?" she asked. Rachel's attention was caught straight away by the pretty, full-skirted floral dress that Mrs Tate was wearing.

"Oh my, what a beautiful dress!" Rachel gasped.

Mrs Tate looked pleased. "Thank you, Rachel," she said.

"My mum made that dress herself!" Kirsty explained proudly. "She added those tiny little buttons down the front of the dress, and sewed in all those pleats."

Mrs Tate laughed. "I've been taking sewing classes," she told Rachel.

"Oh, Mum," Kirsty said with a frown. "I think I need your sewing skills right now!" She'd just noticed that one of the pearly buttons on her shirt had worked loose and was hanging by a single thread.

"I have my sewing box with me – I

can fix that easily," said Mrs Tate.

The girls followed her into the bedroom next door where she opened her sewing box. She took out a reel of white cotton, a needle and a small, round silver object.

"I know that's called a thimble," Rachel remarked, "But I don't know what it's for!"

"It protects my finger when I push the needle through the cloth," Mrs Tate explained. "I'll just thread the needle first."

Kirsty's mum held the needle up and attempted to insert the end of the cotton through the eye. It wouldn't go through. She tried again and again, even moving over to the window for extra light. But it was no use – she couldn't do it.

"Let me have a go," Kirsty offered.
She took the needle and cotton and
tried to push the thread through the
eye. But somehow the cotton kept
missing, even though Kirsty held the
needle very still. Rachel also had a go,
but this time the cotton got into a
tangle and broke.

"Oh, don't worry, Mum," Kirsty said at last. "I'll just change my shirt and you can mend it later."

"Well, making my dress was easy-peasy compared to sewing on that button!" Mrs Tate said, shaking her head. "I seem to be all fingers and thumbs today."

Kirsty glanced at Rachel. They both knew *exactly* why Mrs Tate was having such trouble.

"It's because the goblins have Zadie the Sewing Fairy's magical thimble!"

Rachel whispered as they headed back
to Kirsty's bedroom.

"We *must* find it," Kirsty said
anxiously. "I wonder if we'll see one of
the Magical Crafts Fairies today?"

She opened the wardrobe doors and
gave a little cry of surprise as Zadie the
Sewing Fairy fluttered out!

Not Sew Easy!

Zadie hovered in front of Rachel and Kirsty, a big smile lighting up her face. She was dressed in stylish shorts and purple leggings, with a sparkly pink waistcoat over a white t-shirt.

"I guess you've been expecting me, girls," Zadie said. "You already know I urgently need your help to find my magical thimble or no one will be able to sew *anything,* anywhere!" She sighed. "I can't bear to think of it!"

"Where shall we start looking?" asked Kirsty.

Rachel grabbed the Crafts Week brochure from her bedside table and flicked through it. "It says here that Artemis Johnson is holding a sewing workshop in the market square," Rachel pointed out. "Maybe we should start there?"

"Artie Johnson is the Crafts Week organiser," Kirsty explained to Zadie.

"I think that would be a great place to start!" Zadie said eagerly. "Let's go after breakfast."

"Oops, I almost forgot!" Kirsty said with a grin as Zadie tucked herself neatly into Rachel's pocket, folding her wings away. "I *must* change my shirt."

As soon as Kirsty had swapped her pink shirt for a white one, the girls ran downstairs. Quickly they ate some cereal and then asked to be excused.

"I expect you're keen to get to your next crafts activity," Mr Tate said, looking at them over his newspaper. "What is it today?"

"Sewing," Kirsty and Rachel chorused.

"Oh, I'm *sew* pleased for you!" Kirsty's dad grinned. "Get it?"

The girls laughed. A few moments later they left Mimosa Cottage and headed straight towards the town.

"Girls, I can almost feel an invisible

silken thread *pulling* me towards my
magical thimble!" Zadie whispered as
they approached the market square. "I'm
more sure than ever that we'll find it
here somewhere."

The market square was full of stalls
selling fabrics, cotton thread and other
sewing accessories such as buttons, zips
and ribbons. Kirsty and Rachel were
fascinated by the heaps of shimmering
fabrics in every shade under the sun, and
the big reels of shiny coloured ribbons.

One stall had trays of antique buttons made of wood, porcelain and green jade. The girls kept a sharp eye out for Zadie's thimble among the sewing stuff, but they didn't see it, nor did they spot any goblins.

In the middle of the square was a long wooden table where the sewing workshop was taking place. There was a large group of children seated at the table piled with fabrics and threads.

Artie was moving around from one to the other, checking on the progress of their individual projects. As Rachel and Kirsty went over, Artie spotted them and waved.

"Girls, good to see you again!" she said happily. "Come and join us." She indicated two empty chairs. "Sewing is my *very* favourite craft, you know," Artie went on. "I'm hoping a sewing project will win a prize at the end of Crafts Week." She handed the girls some patterns. "Do have a look through these projects and tell me which one you'd like to try."

Rachel chose a shoulder bag with a
big velvet flower attached to the front,
and Kirsty decided to make a teddy
bear. Then Artie helped them select their
materials – green and purple velvet for
Rachel, and some gold fur fabric for
Kirsty's teddy.

"No sign of goblins yet," Zadie
murmured from inside Rachel's pocket
as the girls cut out their pattern pieces.
"Keep looking, girls!"

Rachel and Kirsty began to sew, but very soon it became clear that things were going wrong all around them. There were cries of dismay from the other children as fabric ripped, threads snapped, zips got stuck and buttons that had been sewn on tightly simply fell off. Artie was running around trying to help everyone and looking very harassed.

Kirsty began stuffing her teddy bear, but to her horror the seams she'd just sewn so carefully came apart and all the stuffing fell out.

Rachel finished attaching the strap of her shoulder bag, but as soon as she put the bag down on the table, it fell off again.

"Oh, this sewing workshop is a total disaster!" Artie groaned.

No Green to be Seen!

Rachel could feel Zadie moving around uneasily in her pocket and guessed that the little fairy was very upset about what was happening. Then a boy sitting opposite the girls suddenly gave a yelp of surprise.

"Where did my silky green fabric disappear to?" the boy said, hunting around on the table. "It was here a minute ago!"

"It probably just got buried under the other stuff," Artie told him.

Rachel reached for some green velvet to make a new strap for her shoulder bag, but, to her amazement, it was snatched away from right under her nose!

"Where did that green velvet go?" Rachel exclaimed, bewildered.

Kirsty was choosing some buttons to make eyes for her teddy bear. But when she leaned over to pick up two green buttons, she found herself grasping at thin air.

"All the green things keep disappearing!" Rachel murmured. "There's no green fabric, cotton, buttons, ribbons or zips left."

"It *must* be something to do with the

goblins," said Kirsty. "After all, green is their favourite colour! But why didn't we see them?"

The girls looked around for goblins. They couldn't see any, but Rachel did spot a trail of green fabric, ribbons, zips and buttons leading across the market square.

"They went that way!" she whispered to Kirsty, pointing out the trail.

Both girls jumped up from their chairs.

"We're just going to look around the stalls for some bits and pieces for our projects," Rachel told Artie. "We'll be back soon."

"That's fine," said Artie.

The girls rushed off. As soon as they were out of sight behind a market stall, Zadie zoomed out of Rachel's pocket.

"Well done for spotting that trail of green, girls!" she cried. "Let's fly around and look for goblins."

Zadie waved her wand and surrounded Rachel and Kirsty with sparkling fairy magic. The girls felt themselves becoming smaller until they were the same size as Zadie, with their own shiny fairy wings.

Quickly Zadie fluttered out from behind the stall. Rachel and Kirsty followed and together the three friends flew through the market, keeping out of sight from the shoppers while they searched for goblins. They darted over, under and between the lengths of multi-coloured fabric that hung over the tops of the stalls, billowing in the breeze. All the time they were looking for any signs of goblin activity.

Suddenly Kirsty spotted an enormous bundle of green fabric which appeared to be moving quickly through the market square all by itself.

"How strange!" Kirsty exclaimed, pointing it out to Rachel and Zadie. "We ought to take a look."

Zadie and the girls swooped down closer to the bundle of material. As they did so, Rachel noticed a pair of enormous, shiny green shoes almost hidden beneath the swathes of fabric.

"There's a goblin under there!" Rachel whispered.

"That must be how he managed to steal all the green things from our sewing workshop," Kirsty murmured, "By hiding under layers of fabric!"

"He's heading to that quiet corner over there," Zadie said, pointing with her wand.

The goblin was hurrying to the outskirts of the market towards a stall half hidden behind a couple of flower arrangements in big pots. Rachel, Kirsty and Zadie chased after him, taking care to keep out of sight.

The stall was already heaped with green fabric, buttons, zips, ribbons and threads, but the goblin began adding the things he'd been carrying to the already teetering pile.

"Look, there are more of them!" Kirsty whispered as she noticed three other goblins close by.

The goblins were having fun with fabric. One was making a tent out of gleaming green satin, while the other two were playing tug-of-war with a long length of emerald-green silk.

Very quietly, Zadie, Rachel and Kirsty flew over to perch on the awning above the stall.

"I wonder which of these goblins has my magic thimble," Zadie said. "We're very close now, girls. I can feel my thimble's magic!"

It was then that Kirsty noticed someone else strutting around below them.

"Who's this?" Kirsty murmured, raising her eyebrows as she stared at his lurid green pin-striped suit and enormous green felt hat. But the brim of the hat was pulled down very low and Kirsty couldn't see the face underneath it.

"Look at his shoes!" Zadie whispered, and the girls saw the same large, shiny green shoes that the goblins were wearing.

"He's a goblin too."

"I sewed this outfit all by myself!" the goblin in the suit was boasting to the others. "I made everything, even this little green handkerchief in my jacket pocket. How clever I am! I can sew *anything*."

Rachel, Kirsty and Zadie exchanged knowing glances.

"That goblin has my magical thimble - that's why he can sew so well!" Zadie declared. "But how do we get it back?"

Goblin Tailor

"That goblin's very proud of his sewing skills," Kirsty said thoughtfully. "Maybe we can use that to get the thimble from him?" And she whispered her plan to Rachel and Zadie.

"Good thinking, Kirsty!" Zadie said. "Let's give it a try."

Swiftly the three of them flew down behind the market stall and out of sight.

There Zadie restored the girls to their
normal size with her magic, and then
she hid herself away in Rachel's pocket.
Kirsty and Rachel strolled casually out
from behind the stall and headed towards
the goblin in the suit.

"Oh!" Rachel exclaimed loudly. All the
goblins turned to stare suspiciously at the
girls. "What a *wonderful* suit! I love it!"

A big, smug grin spread across the goblin's green face. "Isn't it just?" he said proudly. "I made it myself, you know. Every single stitch!"

"That's amazing," Kirsty joined in. "You must be an *incredible* tailor!"

" I am!" the goblin boasted. "I'm a sewing genius!"

"Oh, please could you teach me and my friend to sew just like you?" Rachel pleaded breathlessly, "*Please?*"

The goblin looked very flattered. "Well, you'll never be as brilliant as *me*," he said, "But I suppose I could give you some lessons."

The goblin whisked some needles, thread and fabric from the stall, and then he sat down on the rim of one of the big flowerpots. The girls did the same. Meanwhile the other goblins went back to their games.

"Here, thread your needles," the goblin told them, and he handed them each a reel of cotton and a needle. As Kirsty took the needle from him, she gave a little scream, pretending that she'd pricked herself with the sharp point.

"Ow, that hurt!" Kirsty gasped. "I'm so clumsy!" She glanced innocently at the goblin. "Do you have a thimble I can borrow to protect my finger?"

"No, I don't," the goblin snapped. "Hurry up and thread your needles – I don't have all day, you know!"

Kirsty glanced at Rachel in dismay as the goblin began stroking his jacket lovingly. "Look at this intricate embroidery on the lapels," the goblin sighed with delight. "And see how perfectly straight all the hems are? This is the most beautiful suit in the whole world!" But then he frowned. "It just needs one little finishing touch…"

"What's that?" asked Kirsty. Although her idea hadn't worked, she was still hoping there was some way they could retrieve Zadie's thimble.

"A fabulous swirly cape, just like Jack Frost's!" the goblin declared. He dashed over to the market stall and began rooting through the piles of fabric. "None of this is good enough," he muttered in disgust.

"What kind of fabric are you looking for?" Rachel said.

"I want my cape to be bright green, just like me," the goblin replied, "And very sparkly on the outside, but oh-so-soft on the inside."

A plan popped instantly into Rachel's head. "I've seen some special fabric exactly like that!" she announced. "We'll get it for you."

"Hurrah!" the goblin cheered, and he began tap-dancing happily around in his big shiny green shoes.

The girls dashed off behind the market stall again, and Zadie whizzed out of Rachel's pocket.

"Zadie, you heard what the goblin said," Rachel whispered, "Can you magic up the soft, sparkly fabric he described? I have an idea!"

Thimble Fumble

"Sparkly on the outside, soft on the inside," Zadie repeated with a smile. "Yes, I can do that!"

She swished her wand in the air and the girls saw a misty cloud of magical fairy dust floating around them. Instantly a long length of beautiful, vivid green fabric appeared out of thin air and floated down into Rachel and Kirsty's arms. The fabric was the exact same shade as the goblin's skin and shot through with thin gold threads that sparkled in the sunlight.

"It's gorgeous!" Kirsty exclaimed.

"And it's so *soft*," Rachel added, stroking the underside of the delicate fabric. "He will love it!"

Kirsty folded up the fabric while Zadie dived back into Rachel's pocket. Then they hurried back to the goblin.

"Here we are!" Kirsty said, showing off the fabric with a flourish.

"Oh, how beautiful!" the goblin gasped, wide-eyed. He reached out and gently stroked the fabric. "It's so soft. It's exactly what I want."

He tried to take the fabric, but Kirsty

whisked it out of his reach.

"You can only have it if you return Zadie's magical thimble," she said firmly.

The goblin's face darkened. "No, I'm not giving it to you!" he shouted, and he tried to grab the fabric again. But the girls were ready for him. Kirsty dodged neatly out of his way. Quickly she began circling the goblin and winding the sparkling green fabric around him. Rachel took the other end of the fabric and between them the girls wrapped the goblin up from his shoulders to his feet like an Egyptian mummy.

"We know you have Zadie's thimble,"
Kirsty told the trussed-up goblin. "Now,
where is it?"

"Shan't tell you!" the goblin snapped,
squirming desperately to free himself. But
as he wriggled about trying to escape, his
hat fell off and Rachel
spotted something
shimmering with
fairy magic on top
of his head.

"It's Zadie's
thimble!"
Rachel gasped.

Immediately Zadie flew out of Rachel's
pocket and zoomed directly towards the
thimble perched on the goblin's big green
head. But before she could reach it, the
goblin began yelling loudly.

"A pesky fairy is trying to steal my magical thimble!" he shouted to the others, who'd been too busy playing to notice what had been going on.

Immediately, they all came racing over. Rachel, Kirsty and Zadie tried desperately to grab the thimble first, but the goblin hopped around, trying to avoid them as best as he could. Then, to the girls' dismay, one of the other goblins made a giant leap forward and grabbed the thimble from the top of the goblin's head.

All the goblins whooped with triumph.

"We have to keep this magical object safe for Jack Frost!" the goblin with the thimble declared. He glared at Rachel, Kirsty and Zadie. "*You* can't have it!"

"That thimble's *mine!*" said the goblin in the suit, wriggling out of the green fabric. He tried to snatch the thimble from the other goblin, but he wouldn't give it up. "I need it, or I won't be able to sew my beautiful clothes any more."

"You've had your turn," snapped the goblin with the thimble. "Now *I* want a go!"

"And me! And me!" the other goblins chorused, and they began arguing loudly.

Their squabbling gave Kirsty an idea, and she murmured a few words to Zadie and Rachel. Zadie nodded and pointed her wand at a scrap of green velvet lying on the market stall. A few magical sparkles instantly transformed the velvet into a gorgeous embroidered waistcoat with a green satin lining.

The goblin with the thimble saw the waistcoat and his face lit up. "Oh, I wish I could make lovely clothes like this!" he sighed, grabbing the waistcoat and slipping it on. "And I can, now that the magical thimble is mine!"

The other goblins began yelling angrily at him again.

"It's not yours, it's Jack Frost's!"

"I want to have a go! I want to make myself a beautiful green waistcoat!"

"Give me that thimble back right now – I had it first!"

"Wait!" Rachel stepped in front of them. "*None* of you will be able to sew beautiful clothes if you keep arguing and fighting over the thimble like this!"

She looked at the goblins, who were all staring sullenly back at her. "Listen, Zadie will show you *all* how to make beautiful clothes. She'll teach you how to sew – but only if you give her the magical thimble."

Sewing
Superstars!

The goblin with the thimble frowned.
He glanced at the other goblins, who
were all looking interested in what
Rachel was saying.

"If we give the thimble to Jack Frost,
we'll *never* learn how to sew!" the goblin
in the suit pointed out.

The goblin holding the thimble stroked his waistcoat thoughtfully. Then he nodded. "All right," he agreed, a little reluctantly, and he offered the thimble to Zadie. With a cry of relief, the little fairy swooped towards him. The instant Zadie touched the thimble, it became fairy-sized, and she popped it straight onto her finger, a big smile on her face.

"Thank you," Zadie told the goblins, "But we won't start our sewing lessons now, because you shouldn't have stolen my thimble in the first place!"
The goblins began protesting loudly, but Zadie held up her wand for silence. "We'll start our lessons as soon as I've returned my thimble to Fairyland," she said firmly. "But in the meantime…"

Rachel and Kirsty smiled as another

burst of fairy magic from Zadie's wand
conjured up matching green waistcoats
for all the other goblins. The goblins
whooped with delight as they put the
waistcoats on and they walked off,
preening themselves. Zadie laughed and
flew back to Rachel and Kirsty.

"It's time for me to go home now,"
Zadie said happily. "Girls, saying thank
you just doesn't seem to be enough!
You've been complete superstars, and
everyone in Fairyland is going to be so
thrilled when I tell them how you've
helped us once
again. Goodbye,
and see you
very soon!"

"Goodbye,"
the girls called
as Zadie
disappeared
in a shower
of sparkles,
waving her
thimble at them
in farewell.

"Let's take all these green things back to Artie's workshop," Rachel suggested, pointing at the goblins' stall.

Quickly the girls gathered everything up and hurried through the market square. When they arrived at the workshop, both of them were relieved to see that everyone, including Artie, was looking a lot happier.

"Girls, our sewing projects are back on track!" Artie called to them. "And what a wonderful haul of sewing stuff you've collected."

"Everything's OK now that Zadie has her thimble again," Rachel whispered to Kirsty, picking up her half-finished shoulder bag.

"At least now my poor little teddy won't lose his insides!" Kirsty joked.

Later that day, the girls rushed back to Mimosa Cottage, eager to show Mrs Tate their sewing projects.

"What a gorgeous shoulder bag, Rachel!" Mrs Tate exclaimed, "I love the velvet flower on the front. And that's such a sweet little teddy, Kirsty. Well done, both of you."

Rachel and Kirsty beamed proudly at each other.

"I've been working on a sewing project of my own while you've been gone," Mrs Tate went on, and she handed each of the girls a beautiful pink art apron with purple ribbon ties.

"Oh, Mum, these are brilliant!" Kirsty gasped. "Look, Rachel, our names are embroidered on the front."

"I love it!" Rachel declared, trying her

apron on immediately. "We can wear them whenever we do arts and crafts, Kirsty."

"I'm glad you like them," said Mrs Tate with a smile. "Now, shall I have another go at sewing that loose button on your shirt, Kirsty?"

But Kirsty shook her head. "No, thanks, Mum. Now that Rachel and I have learnt to sew, we're going to do it ourselves," she said.

The girls ran upstairs to Kirsty's bedroom, still admiring their aprons. But when Kirsty took the shirt from her wardrobe, she gave a cry of surprise.

"Rachel, look! The button's already been sewn on - with *really* sparkly thread!"

"Fairy magic!" Rachel

laughed. "And see, there's something else – a special, sparkly message from Zadie, stitched inside the hem of the shirt."

"It says *thank you*." Kirsty grinned at her friend. "Isn't that amazing, Rachel? I'm so glad we helped another of the fairies find their magical crafts object."

"And let's hope we can find the others in time to save Crafts Week from total disaster!" added Rachel.

The End

**Now it's time for Kirsty and
Rachel to help...**

Josie the Jewellery-Making Fairy

Read on for a sneak peek...

Rachel Walker sat up and yawned,
then smiled as she remembered where
she was. It was early in the morning,
but the warmth of the sun was already
soaking through the canvas of her tent.
She looked across at her best friend
Kirsty Tate, who was still curled up
in her sleeping bag. So far their stay
on Rainspell Island had been full of
adventure.

"I wonder what today will bring," she
whispered to herself.

Rachel leaned back on her pillow and
thought about all the things that had

happened since they arrived. It was Craft Week on the island, and so far the girls had tried pottery, drawing and sewing. There were plenty more crafts left to try, as well as a competition and exhibition at the end of the week. Things had got even more exciting when they met Kayla the Pottery Fairy.

Read **Josie the Jewellery-Making Fairy** to find out what adventures are in store for Kirsty and Rachel!

Meet the
Magical Crafts Fairies

Jack Frost has stolen the Magical Crafts Fairies' special objects. Can Kirsty and Rachel help get them back before Rainspell Island's Crafts Week is ruined?

www.rainbowmagicbooks.co.uk

Competition!

The Magical Crafts Fairies have created a special
competition just for you!
In the back of each book in the Magical Crafts series there
will be a question for you to answer.
First you need to collect the answer from the back
of each book in the series.
Once you have all the answers, take the first letter from
each one and arrange them to spell a secret word!
When you have the answer, go online and enter!

What is Rachel's surname?

_ _ _ _ _ _

We will put all the correct entries into a draw and select
a winner to receive a special Rainbow Magic Goody Bag
featuring lots of treats for you and your fairy friends.
You'll also star in a new Rainbow Magic story!

Enter online now at www.rainbowmagicbooks.co.uk

Have you read them all?

The Rainbow Fairies
1. Ruby the Red Fairy ☐
2. Amber the Orange Fairy ☐
3. Saffron the Yellow Fairy ☐
4. Fern the Green Fairy ☐
5. Sky the Blue Fairy ☐
6. Izzy the Indigo Fairy ☐
7. Heather the Violet Fairy ☐

The Weather Fairies
8. Crystal the Snow Fairy ☐
9. Abigail the Breeze Fairy ☐
10. Pearl the Cloud Fairy ☐
11. Goldie the Sunshine Fairy ☐
12. Evie the Mist Fairy ☐
13. Storm the Lightning Fairy ☐
14. Hayley the Rain Fairy ☐

The Party Fairies
15. Cherry the Cake Fairy ☐
16. Melodie the Music Fairy ☐
17. Grace the Glitter Fairy ☐
18. Honey the Sweet Fairy ☐
19. Polly the Party Fun Fairy ☐
20. Phoebe the Fashion Fairy ☐
21. Jasmine the Present Fairy ☐

The Jewel Fairies
22. India the Moonstone Fairy ☐
23. Scarlett the Garnet Fairy ☐
24. Emily the Emerald Fairy ☐
25. Chloe the Topaz Fairy ☐
26. Amy the Amethyst Fairy ☐
27. Sophie the Sapphire Fairy ☐
28. Lucy the Diamond Fairy ☐

The Pet Keeper Fairies
29. Katie the Kitten Fairy ☐
30. Bella the Bunny Fairy ☐
31. Georgia the Guinea Pig Fairy ☐
32. Lauren the Puppy Fairy ☐
33. Harriet the Hamster Fairy ☐
34. Molly the Goldfish Fairy ☐
35. Penny the Pony Fairy ☐

The Fun Day Fairies
36. Megan the Monday Fairy
37. Tallulah the Tuesday Fairy
38. Willow the Wednesday Fairy
39. Thea the Thursday Fairy
40. Freya the Friday Fairy
41. Sienna the Saturday Fairy
42. Sarah the Sunday Fairy

The Petal Fairies
43. Tia the Tulip Fairy
44. Pippa the Poppy Fairy
45. Louise the Lily Fairy
46. Charlotte the Sunflower Fairy
47. Olivia the Orchid Fairy
48. Danielle the Daisy Fairy
49. Ella the Rose Fairy

The Dance Fairies
50. Bethany the Ballet Fairy
51. Jade the Disco Fairy
52. Rebecca the Rock'n'Roll Fairy
53. Tasha the Tap Dance Fairy
54. Jessica the Jazz Fairy
55. Saskia the Salsa Fairy
56. Imogen the Ice Dance Fairy

The Sporty Fairies
57. Helena the Horseriding Fairy
58. Francesca the Football Fairy
59. Zoe the Skating Fairy
60. Naomi the Netball Fairy
61. Samantha the Swimming Fairy
62. Alice the Tennis Fairy
63. Gemma the Gymnastics Fairy

The Music Fairies
64. Poppy the Piano Fairy
65. Ellie the Guitar Fairy
66. Fiona the Flute Fairy
67. Danni the Drum Fairy
68. Maya the Harp Fairy
69. Victoria the Violin Fairy
70. Sadie the Saxophone Fairy

The Magical Animal Fairies
71. Ashley the Dragon Fairy ☐
72. Lara the Black Cat Fairy ☐
73. Erin the Firebird Fairy ☐
74. Rihanna the Seahorse Fairy ☐
75. Sophia the Snow Swan Fairy ☐
76. Leona the Unicorn Fairy ☐
77. Caitlin the Ice Bear Fairy ☐

The Green Fairies
78. Nicole the Beach Fairy ☐
79. Isabella the Air Fairy ☐
80. Edie the Garden Fairy ☐
81. Coral the Reef Fairy ☐
82. Lily the Rainforest Fairy ☐
83. Carrie the Snow Cap Fairy ☐
84. Milly the River Fairy ☐

The Ocean Fairies
85. Ally the Dolphin Fairy ☐
86. Amelie the Seal Fairy ☐
87. Pia the Penguin Fairy ☐
88. Tess the Sea Turtle Fairy ☐
89. Stephanie the Starfish Fairy ☐
90. Whitney the Whale Fairy ☐
91. Courtney the Clownfish Fairy ☐

The Twilight Fairies
92. Ava the Sunset Fairy ☐
93. Lexi the Firefly Fairy ☐
94. Zara the Starlight Fairy ☐
95. Morgan the Midnight Fairy ☐
96. Yasmin the Night Owl Fairy ☐
97. Maisie the Moonbeam Fairy ☐
98. Sabrina the Sweet Dreams Fairy ☐

The Showtime Fairies
99. Madison the Magic Show Fairy ☐
100. Leah the Theatre Fairy ☐
101. Alesha the Acrobat Fairy ☐
102. Darcey the Dance Diva Fairy ☐
103. Taylor the Talent Show Fairy ☐
104. Amelia the Singing Fairy ☐
105. Isla the Ice Star Fairy ☐

The Princess Fairies
106. Honor the Happy Days Fairy ☐
107. Demi the Dressing-Up Fairy ☐
108. Anya the Cuddly Creatures Fairy ☐
109. Elisa the Adventure Fairy ☐
110. Lizzie the Sweet Treats Fairy ☐
111. Maddie the Playtime Fairy ☐
112. Eva the Enchanted Ball Fairy ☐

The Pop Star Fairies
113. Jessie the Lyrics Fairy ☐
114. Adele the Singing Coach Fairy ☐
115. Vanessa the Dance Steps Fairy ☐
116. Miley the Stylist Fairy ☐
117. Frankie the Make-Up Fairy ☐
118. Rochelle the Star Spotter Fairy ☐
119. Una the Concert Fairy ☐

The Fashion Fairies
120. Miranda the Beauty Fairy ☐
121. Claudia the Accessories Fairy ☐
122. Tyra the Dress Designer Fairy ☐
123. Alexa the Fashion Reporter Fairy ☐
124. Matilda the Hair Stylist Fairy ☐
125. Brooke the Photographer Fairy ☐
126. Lola the Fashion Fairy ☐

The Sweet Fairies
127. Lottie the Lollipop Fairy ☐
128. Esme the Ice Cream Fairy ☐
129. Coco the Cupcake Fairy ☐
130. Clara the Chocolate Fairy ☐
131. Madeleine the Cookie Fairy ☐
132. Layla the Candyfloss Fairy ☐
133. Nina the Birthday Cake Fairy ☐

The Baby Animal Rescue Fairies
134. Mae the Panda Fairy ☐
135. Kitty the Tiger Fairy ☐
136. Mara the Meerkat Fairy ☐
137. Savannah the Zebra Fairy ☐
138. Kimberley the Koala Fairy ☐
139. Rosie the Honey Bear Fairy ☐
140. Anna the Arctic Fox Fairy ☐

The Magical Crafts Fairies
141. Kayla the Pottery Fairy ☐
142. Annabelle the Drawing Fairy ☐
143. Zadie the Sewing Fairy ☐
144. Josie the Jewellery-Making Fairy ☐
145. Violet the Painting Fairy ☐
146. Libby the Story-Writing Fairy ☐
147. Roxie the Baking Fairy ☐

There's a book of fairy fun for everyone!

www.rainbowmagicbooks.co.uk

Lila & Myla
the Twins
Fairies

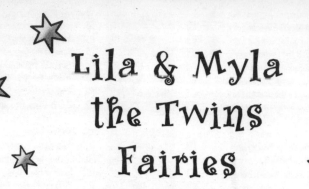

**Meet Lila and Myla the Twins Fairies!
Can the fairies stop Jack Frost before he uses
their magic to create his very own twin?**

www.rainbowmagicbooks.co.uk